FLYY GIRLS

MICAH: THE GOOD GIRL

BY ASHLEY WOODFOLK

PENGUIN WORKSHOP

TO BELLA. SHINE BRIGHT, BABY GIRL—AW

PENGUIN WORKSHOP
An Imprint of Penguin Random House LLC, New York

Text copyright © 2020 by Ashwin Writing LLC. Illustrations copyright © 2020 by Penguin Random House LLC. All rights reserved. Published by Penguin Workshop, an imprint of Penguin Random House LLC, New York. PENGUIN and PENGUIN WORKSHOP are trademarks of Penguin Books Ltd, and the W colophon is a registered trademark of Penguin Random House LLC. Printed in the USA.

Visit us online at www.penguinrandomhouse.com.

Cover illustration by Zharia Shinn

Library of Congress Cataloging-in-Publication Data is available upon request.

ISBN 9780593096048 (pbk)
ISBN 9780593096055 (hc)

10 9 8 7 6 5 4 3 2 1
10 9 8 7 6 5 4 3 2 1

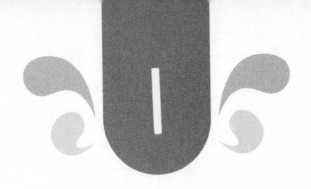

Flashing red lights. The piercing scream of a siren. The sharp smell of rubber and asphalt. The polluted New York air was thick with humidity and it wasn't even July yet.

The ambulance Micah Dupree heard was trying to make its way past her, on to some emergency. But even though she remained perfectly safe, Micah couldn't stop sweating. Her pulse was racing and her chest felt tight. The ambulance would have normally sped by in seconds, but the bumper-to-bumper traffic on Canal Street kept the siren blaring loudly in the same spot for several long minutes.

She squeezed her eyes shut and covered her ears, but she could still hear the high-pitched noise of it. The sound reminded her of a day she was always trying to forget.

She attempted to slow her breathing, but nothing worked. She bent forward and focused on the laces in her shoes, but her eyes kept blurring with tears. Micah couldn't breathe. It felt like she might die.

"You good?" some stranger asked when she dropped her bag and staggered to sit on the closest curb.

"Uh-huh," Micah mumbled.

She reached for her phone with sweaty hands. She needed to call Ty, to hear his calm, reassuring voice, but he still didn't know about her panic attacks. Micah worried that he wouldn't feel the same way about her if he knew, so for now she wanted to keep them a secret. She typed out a message to Noelle Lee. She was almost certain her friend would be working at her grandparents' nearby restaurant. Noelle was the only member of the Flyy Girls, and really the only person period, who she trusted with the truth.

It's happening, Micah typed. *Can you come?*

Noelle texted back instantly. *You're sooo lucky. Mei just came in for her shift, so I should be able to sneak away. Where you at?*

Minutes later, Noelle sat down beside Micah on the curb and handed her a bottle of water. She lifted Micah's hand and put it on her chest, and told her to breathe.

"In and out," Noelle said. "Yeah, just like that. It's okay. Slower. Breathe with me. It's all right, don't cry. You're doing so good."

When it finally ended, it felt like the panic

attack hadn't even happened. Now Micah couldn't stop laughing at Noelle's story about the family who came into the restaurant with a baby who pooped through his onesie and knocked over an untouched order of chow fun.

But because she lived in New York City, Micah knew the next ambulance (and the next attack) could be right around the corner, literally. She still felt a little on edge all the time.

It made her paranoid. It made her want a different brain and body. But she knew that wasn't possible, so she was trying to cope with what she had.

Micah hadn't always felt like this. But last summer changed everything. Now the sound of an emergency vehicle made her freak out. If it passed her quickly enough, she'd just get sweaty palms or shake a bit, feeling weak in the knees. But if not—if she and the ambulance

had to spend any time sharing the same space—
she panicked.

"Are they happening less, at least?" Noelle
asked.

"They had been, but ever since it started
getting hot out, it's been reminding me more of
the day it happened."

Noelle nodded. "That makes sense. You still
seeing that doctor?"

"Every Tuesday," Micah said.

"Is it helping?"

"Not sure."

"Yeah. Therapy helped Pierre a little. But he
still has them if he gets too overwhelmed."

This was why Micah always called Noelle
when her body went haywire. Noelle's little
brother deals with anxiety, so panic attacks
didn't freak her out like they would Tobyn.
And Micah thought Lux might just tell her to

pull it together. Micah's parents didn't even like admitting she had anxiety issues—they ignored it, and so she tried to, too. But Noelle knew exactly how to help.

"On your way to work?" Noelle asked, and Micah nodded. "Gonna see Ty?" she asked next, kinda singing the words. Micah couldn't help but grin, but then Noelle's face turned serious. "He know about these? Or about the fact that they're happening more lately?"

Micah didn't want to think about next month's anniversary. It hovered over this whole summer like a cloud threatening rain. She didn't want to talk about it with Noelle, and she definitely didn't want to tell Ty. He knew about what happened last summer, but she didn't want him to know she couldn't hear a siren without losing it.

"No. I don't want to bother him with all the

drama." She had something more important on her mind when it came to Ty, anyway.

Noelle shrugged, opened her bag, and handed Micah what looked like a small yellow pie. The sweet egg tart with a flaky crust was Micah's favorite Chinese dessert.

"Well, for now," Noelle said, "keep calm and eat daan taat."

Micah grinned and grabbed the pastry. "Whatever you say."

Miraculously, after she thanked Noelle for coming to her rescue, Micah made it to church without another incident. Triumphant Kingdom A.M.E. Church was the only place Micah could spend any real time other than school. She attended service every Sunday,

Bible study every Wednesday, and sometimes went to a prayer service or two during the rest of the week. So the church-run camp was the only place her parents would ever hear of her working in the summer. Her boyfriend, Ty, went to the same church and worked at the camp, too. She couldn't wait to see him. When she spotted the back of his head through one of the stained-glass windows, she took the steps two at a time up to the front door.

Since they'd first discovered they could get away with it, she and Tyriq Valentine had risked sneaking into the church's back parking lot to make out while the littlest campers took their naps. They were supposed to be on their "lunch break," but the only thing they tasted when they stole away for the hour was each other.

If they were ever found out, it would not

go well. For one, they were both well known enough at the church that their parents would definitely hear about it. Whether the news came through gossiping church members or from a church elder telling her mom and dad directly, Micah could imagine her mother's stern tsks and her father's disapproving frown followed by a quick and severe punishment. And since they were supposed to be working, doing anything that wasn't work—and making out definitely counted as *not work*—might even get them fired. Maybe worst of all, they both wore promise rings—silver bands they'd been given two years ago when they promised during a Sunday service to wait to have sex until they were married. Making out in a back parking lot wasn't sex, of course, but Micah knew from experience that church folks had a way of jumping to conclusions. Micah couldn't imagine being caught, so she tried to be careful.

The only problem? Ty Valentine was an excellent kisser, and Micah sometimes found herself being a little more reckless. Today, for instance, she touched his face when she thought no one would see. She'd been so relieved to hear his soft voice after the morning she'd had that she couldn't help it. A few hours later, she slipped her finger into his back pocket and yanked him closer to her while the campers were lining up to walk to a nearby playground for recess. And when naptime for the youngest kids at camp came around, she grabbed and held on to his hand before they'd even made it to the church's side door.

Ty used his hands a lot when they kissed, which Micah loved. He cupped her cheeks and held the back of her neck, and he never reached for her hair because he knew better.

He was the only boy she'd ever kissed, and secretly Micah hoped he'd be the only one forever. She couldn't imagine feeling this way about anyone other than Ty, whose pretty skin was the color of bread crusts, just a hair lighter than her own. He bit her bottom lip a little, and she smiled without breaking contact and kissed him harder. In that moment, she felt a tug on her heart and in her body. She might want to do more with Ty Valentine than kiss him. And soon.

"Do you think . . . ," Micah started saying with some hesitation in her voice, "that abstinence makes sense?" She asked this as soon as Ty broke their kiss, and gave her a chance to catch her breath. "Like, do you think it's realistic for kids like us?"

Ty looked a bit surprised, but this kind of talk wasn't coming out of nowhere for her.

During their makeout sessions, they often got into debates about different things. Sometimes they talked about music, politics, or which new TV show was best. And often they talked about stuff like this: the rules they were supposed to follow and what they *really* thought about it all.

"You've been thinking about this for a while, haven't you?" Ty said. He snaked his arm around her hip and tugged her closer.

"Maybe," Micah muttered. The truth was, she'd been thinking about this since she had her first crush at twelve or thirteen. Even then she could imagine the fluttery feeling in her stomach growing into something like love. She'd been thinking about it more often since last year, when Ty and his family first came to Triumphant Kingdom. When he smiled at her for the first time a few months ago during Communion, and then asked her out right after the service ended, she had so many questions. *How did one date and not kiss? How did one kiss and not do more than that?* Ty promised he'd keep their relationship a secret after she told him she wasn't exactly allowed to date, but she couldn't stop thinking about what it might mean to love someone and how she might want to show it. And now that she'd fallen hard and fast for Ty this summer, the questions had turned into something firm enough to say out loud.

"I guess I've been feeling like some of the stuff Pastor Bridges talks about isn't as black and white as he'd like us to think it is. Like maybe there're shades of gray to all of this."

"Even abstinence?" Ty asked.

"Especially abstinence. Like, do you know anyone who stayed a virgin until they got married other than the weirdos on those reality TV shows who kiss for the first time during their wedding ceremonies?"

Ty laughed. "I guess not. But I think the waiting is about more than just following some random rule. I think it's about sacrifice and discipline, and showing God you love and respect Him and His Word more than the things your body wants."

She loved that he never immediately agreed with her about anything.

"Sure, okay. But what if it's not only something my body wants? Isn't this—sex—supposed to be about love?"

Ty smirked and nodded. "So, what exactly are you saying?"

Micah swallowed hard. All that stuff about lust and sex and sin they learned about in church didn't feel like it applied to her and Ty. Plus, she *wanted* this. She wanted him.

"I guess I'm saying I love you. And I'm not

sure I want to wait."

Ty grinned. He reached for and held both her hands. "Look, you know I've loved you since the day we met," Ty said. "But this is a big risk, Micah. And while I would definitely be down, I don't want us to regret it. Or to get caught."

Micah laughed. "Okay," she said, nodding. She got up on her tiptoes and pushed her lips against his again. "We'll plan it all out, every detail. And I'll think about it a little more, too."

"Even if you decide you really want to do this, shouldn't we wait a little while, anyway? Didn't the accident happen around this time last year?"

Micah's nostrils flared as she thought about ambulances and Noelle and last summer.

"Shut up and kiss me," she said. And Ty listened.

2

"Do we have to talk about this now? It's *summer*," Tobyn Wolfe whined.

Lux Lawson was painting Micah's nails while Tobyn lounged on Lux's living room couch. Micah liked hanging out over here specifically because Lux's little sister was so cute. It also helped that Lux's stepmom gave them the kind of space Micah's parents never would, and Lux's dad was almost never home.

So far, Micah's thumbs were green, her pinkies were pink, and her pointer fingers were yellow. Only Lux painted nails this way—

silently, and from the outside in.

"I just have no idea what to paint for this project," Micah said, talking about the assignment every student at Augusta Savage School of the Arts had to complete the summer before their senior year. "We still have a few weeks to figure something out, but still. It needs to be perfect."

Tobyn rolled her eyes and turned up the music on her phone. "You always say that," she said. "But nothing is ever perfect, boo, sorry to tell ya."

"Easy for you to say," Micah said. "You write songs, like, *all* the time. You just have to pick one. Plus you have a pro musician for a sister to help you!"

Tobyn shrugged. "Devyn probably won't help me, if you want to know the truth. She hated high school and all the assignments.

I doubt she'd volunteer to dive back in."

"Still, it'll be easier for you than me. And mine *needs* to be perfect," Micah insisted. "Help me out. You got any ideas I can steal?"

"Nope. My brain is officially off for the summer. But are we talking about your art project because you don't want to talk about the anniversary?"

Lux selected a bottle of glittery orange nail polish from her collection and stroked it over the nails on both of Micah's ring fingers. She looked up at Micah when she finished a second coat. "Damn, I'm good," Lux said, talking about the manicure. Micah smiled, but she still hadn't answered Tobyn's question.

"What's Noelle doing? I thought she was coming over, too," Micah said to Lux. She didn't look at Tobyn.

Lux picked out one last color, a deep indigo,

before she answered. "Noelle had to help at the restaurant again. And are we really not going to talk about the anniversary?"

Micah didn't want to talk about it. She wanted to pretend it wasn't happening. "Maybe I'll paint Ty," she said, more to herself than to Lux or Tobyn, but they allowed the shift in conversation.

"How are things going with you two?" Tobyn asked, grinning. "Still making out when no one's looking?"

"Yeah," Micah said. She couldn't help but smile. "And I've been thinking about maybe doing more."

"No way," said Tobyn. Her mouth fell open. "Really? This would be your first time, right?"

Micah nodded.

"What does Ty think?"

"He's considering it," Micah said. "He's

worried about us getting caught, but I think he wants to as much as I do."

"Church kids," Lux said, shaking her head. "I swear. You guys talk about virginity so much, but you're freakier than all the kids I know combined."

"Oh, shut up," Micah said. Lux was still the new girl, having transferred to Augusta Savage School of the Arts in the middle of junior year. After she'd been caught lying to them about why she'd transferred, she apologized in a way only a Flyy Girl would: with a pretty epic prank. Now Lux was one of them.

"What we really should be talking about," Lux said, "is the senior prank we need to plan."

Tobyn nodded, agreeing. "But if we talk about that without Noelle, she'd murder us."

"You're not wrong," Micah said. "So let's wait until all *four* of the Flyy Girls are together."

"Speaking of girls, how's that girl of yours doing, Tobyn?" Lux said, and Tobyn told them about the latest fight she and her girlfriend, Ava, had. When Lux chimed in about Emmett, a guy she liked, Micah was so relieved. Because as the girls talked about their own crushes and how unfair it was to have to do their senior project during their summer vacations, all mentions of the dark upcoming anniversary were left behind.

That night, Micah came home to an empty apartment. She dropped her things by the door and headed down the hall to a room no one in her family entered very often. The door creaked slowly open and Micah stood in the doorway for a second before stepping inside.

"Hey, Milo," Micah finally said to the empty room. She kept her voice low, like she would at church. She looked down the hall at the front door behind her and listened, but she heard no jingle of keys, footsteps, or other signs that her parents were around. She stepped inside. The room still looked just as he'd left it.

The walls were plastered with posters of airborne basketball players and long-haired bands Micah had never heard of. There were still clothes in the closet and a collection of sneakers under the bed. Micah touched a brush that still had spirals of dark hair curled around the bristles, and she slipped on a pair of his glasses before glancing into a nearby mirror.

Micah's face was a strange mixture of her parents' features. She had her mother's wide nose and her father's high cheekbones, her mom's pointy chin and her dad's thick hair.

At some angles she looked like them both, and in certain light like neither of them at all. But her brother, Milo, had looked just like her, and there were photos of him all over the apartment.

On the fridge there were pictures of him as a baby and a kindergartner alongside sketches he'd done—sophisticated crayon drawings that showed his early talent. There were black-and-white photos of him as a scrawny kid tucked into the corner of the mirror in her mom's vanity along with clippings from magazines that had featured some of his tween-age masterpieces. And in the hallway there were photographs of him, a thin and tall teen with Micah's eyes but a grin that was all his own, standing proudly beside his work at gallery openings.

"So we have this big project due before the

start of senior year. I'm freaking out about what to do," she said to no one at all. She sat on his bed and ran her fingers across his duvet. "Do you think a painting that incorporated found objects would be cool? Or is that trying too hard?" She glanced over at the mirror again. Looking at her reflection sometimes really felt like looking at her brother. "I can hear you now," Micah said, laughing to herself a bit. Then, in a deeper voice, she muttered, "People gonna think you unoriginal as hell, Mike-Mike." If Milo had heard her bad impression of him, Micah thought, he would have said, *That don't sound nothing like me, big head.*

Micah crossed the room and opened the top drawer of his dresser slowly so she wouldn't make any noise. She knew her parents would be home soon and she didn't want her mom to know she was in here. While her dad might be okay with her hanging out in the room sometimes, she didn't want him to discover her snooping.

"You know this art stuff has never come as easily for me as it did for you, but I've never been this unsure about a painting before. Maybe it's because of everything that's going on with Ty and how I've been feeling in therapy. Maybe it's because ambulances are scaring the crap out of me again."

She dug a little deeper into the drawer, pushing socks and T-shirts aside. His scent, freshly cut grass and spicy deodorant, hit her like a slap in the face. She held her breath for a second, then changed her mind and took a big whiff. "Maybe it's because of what next month is."

She saw the sketchbook beside a well-worn Bible. She'd known the sketchbook was here for nearly a year, but she hadn't opened it since *it* happened. She reached for it.

"Micah?" her mother's voice rang out in the hallway. She must have just gotten home. "Where are you, honey?"

Micah grabbed the sketchbook. She tucked it into the back of her skirt and pulled her shirt down over it.

"Bye, Milo," she said, stepping silently into the hall.

"Coming!" she called to her mom.

In her room that night, Micah paged through Milo's sketchbook. She saw drawings of little kids on the subway and dogs at the park, and dozens of original graffiti tags that would never get thrown up on a wall. There were lots of sketches of Micah laughing or twirling in one of her many skirts, and dozens of her parents, Michelle and Paul Dupree, doing unexciting things like making sandwiches or drinking coffee.

Micah flipped through nearly half of the thick book right there on her bed and paused only when she landed on a self-portrait Milo had drawn. The lines of his thick eyebrows and broad nose made Micah ache.

A few pages later, when she found a sketch of dozens of people on the museum stairs where they used to meet, she slowly closed the book. She'd had enough for one night.

3

TUESDAY, JUNE 30, 4:00 P.M.

Dr. Patel: *So, how are you feeling as we approach the anniversary? How are things at home?*

Micah: *Okay, I guess. Maybe I'm a little anxious.*

Dr. Patel: *Just a little?*

Micah: *To be real with you, I had another panic attack.*

Dr. Patel: *That's the third one in less than a month.*

Micah: *I know.*

Dr. Patel: *Are ambulances still your main trigger?*

Micah: *Yeah, but I think if I wasn't taking that medicine, this would all be worse.*

Dr. Patel: *Did you try calling someone, like we talked about last time?*

Micah: *I called Noelle. And she helped a bit.*

Dr. Patel: *Maybe next time, if there is a next time, try listening to music until you get past the siren.*

Micah: *Ah, like turn it way, way up? Hadn't thought of that. Thanks, Doc. That's a good idea.*

Dr. Patel: *I may talk to your parents about trying a different medication. How are they doing? This has to be a tough time for them, too.*

Micah: *Dad's just getting quiet, the way*

he always does when something he doesn't wanna talk about is happening. Mom's doing that thing where she cleans everything but avoids his room like she'll catch a zombie virus if she even gets close to the door.

Dr. Patel: *I see. And are you still visiting his room in secret?*

Micah: *Sometimes. Mostly when I have questions or I need to talk to someone who gets me.*

Dr. Patel: *What kinds of questions?*

Micah: *Oh, you know. How do I keep Mom's plants alive while she's away on business? He used to do that—water the plants for her. Or, like, why is Dad so obsessed with that one meat loaf recipe, and how does he always screw it up?*

Dr. Patel: [laughs]

Micah: *Or, I guess . . . Is it wrong to want to be close to someone?*

Dr. Patel: *Tell me a little more about that last one.*

Micah: *Ugh. Do I have to?*

Dr. Patel: *You don't have to do anything here, you know that, Micah. But . . .*

Micah: *But it might make things more interesting if I do.*

Dr. Patel: *You'd make my job a little easier, kid.*

Micah: *Well, I guess I've just been thinking a lot about some of the stuff I was raised to believe.*

Dr. Patel: *Say more.*

Micah: *Because of Ty. Because of how we feel about each other. Like, it can't be wrong— to love someone. And I guess I've been thinking about it all more because of Milo, too—because of how he . . . ran out of time.*

Dr. Patel: *I see. And so you have questions about faith?*

Micah: *More like I have questions about . . . sex. Sorry, is this weird?*

Dr. Patel: *Not to me.*

Micah: *Cool. Well, me and Milo never talked about that stuff. But I don't know. Now I wish we had.*

Dr. Patel: *I see. And does going into that room help you answer questions about plants and meat loaf and sex? Or is it more about feeling close to him?*

Micah: *I guess I like imagining what it might have been like, you know? To still have a brother to talk to about all that stuff.*

4

"You have to go?" Lux asked Micah. They were on Micah's rooftop, where they'd hang out year-round if they were able to. They were eating giant ice pops they'd bought at the bodega on the corner and waiting for fireworks. Firecrackers had been popping and sparklers fizzing all afternoon, but the really fun stuff wouldn't start until after sunset. Unfortunately, Micah would probably miss most of it. "You're always at church."

She *was* always at church. Bible study on Wednesdays, regular services on Sunday, plus her job at the camp. And occasionally her parents asked her to go to prayer services on random days, too. Even though it was the Fourth of July, this was one of those days.

"Yes she has to go," Tobyn and Noelle replied in unison. Both of their lips were stained bright red by their cherry ice pops.

"Her mom will flip if she doesn't," Tobyn added.

"I like going," Micah told them, and Noelle rolled her eyes.

"Suuuure you do," she said.

But the truth was, Micah really did. She'd had questions lately about faith and life and how the two were meant to go together, but she liked having something to question and something to believe in. She didn't know how to talk to Noelle, Tobyn, and Lux about that, though.

"Is Ty gonna be there?" Lux asked next.

Her lips were purple from her grape ice pop.

"Probably," Noelle said.

"Oh." Tobyn grinned. "So *that's* why you like going."

"That is not why," Micah said. She pulled her phone out and opened her camera. There was no way the bright blue color on her lips would wear off before she got to the church. It made her cringe to think of Ty seeing her with a weird-colored mouth. She knew her mom would have something to say about it, too. "I mean, that's not the *only* reason why."

They all laughed.

"What's up with you two, anyway?" Tobyn asked. "Any updates?" She'd finished her ice pop and tilted herself forward into a handstand. The girl hated sitting still, and sugar only increased her antsiness. *Tobyn has the same high energy as her sister*, Micah thought, remembering the way Devyn jumped around the stage when they went to see her band perform in the spring.

"Nothing is 'up' with us," Micah said at first. But a minute later, she gave in. She turned to Noelle. "We're thinking about maybe not waiting."

"I'm sorry, what?" Noelle asked. She walked over to where Micah was lounging on one of the roof deck lawn chairs and squinted at Micah hard through her wire-rimmed glasses. "Goody-Goody Micah Dupree is thinking about *not* waiting?"

Micah shielded her eyes and looked up. She shrugged. Then nodded.

"They've been making out all summer," Lux said. She licked a bit of purple syrup that was trickling down her wrist. "This shouldn't be a surprise."

"You're really going to do it, then?" Tobyn asked. She let her legs fall backward before crab-walking closer to her friends.

"She won't," Noelle answered for her. "Because of, you know, *Jesus*." She smirked and Tobyn giggled, and Lux looked like she was waiting for Micah to say something.

Micah's nostrils flared. Noelle could be so sweet, and then in an instant she could turn on you. Micah loved her friend, but she hated her sometimes, too.

"It's not that simple," Micah said.

But Noelle wouldn't stop talking. "The Bible says not to do . . . *that* . . . outside of marriage, right? So if you do it, you're gonna go to hell. And Good-Girl Micah could never do anything that might end in hellfire. Besides, what would Mommy and Daddy say?"

"Don't be a dick, Noelle," Tobyn said.

"What?" Noelle asked innocently.

Micah knew Noelle was right. Until very recently, she had believed the Bible without question. And she and Ty *were* worried about her parents finding out.

But Micah wanted Ty. She didn't know why; she just knew that all of a sudden she felt really ready. But could she be making a mistake?

Micah didn't want to talk about this anymore. She was starting to feel panicky. As she grabbed her bag to leave, Milo's sketchbook fell out.

"What's this?" Noelle asked, snatching it up. She opened the book and started flipping through the pages. "Whoa, Micah. I thought painting was your thing. When'd you get so good at drawing?"

The other girls came over to look through the book, too, and Micah felt her chest starting to get tight like it did when she heard an ambulance—just like it had the other day.

"Give it back," Micah said so quietly that none of the girls heard her.

"Holy shit," Lux said, looking up. "Since when do you do graffiti?" She flipped the book around and pointed to one of Milo's tags. "Or sketches with this much detail?"

"Wow," Tobyn said next. "You've been holding out."

"It's not mine," Micah said. She squeezed her eyes shut and spoke louder. "It's Milo's. Give it back."

"Oh," they all said at the same time. Noelle and Tobyn knew everything about Milo. That her perfect big brother had been on the verge of becoming famous when he died. Lux only knew that his name made Micah go quiet. But they all could see that this book meant something special to her.

Noelle closed the book and handed it back to Micah. "Sorry, boo."

Micah swallowed hard and started tucking it into her bag. Even with the sketchbook now back in her possession, she didn't feel her anxiety fading. As Micah tucked the sketchbook into her bag, she checked the time on her phone and realized she was going to be late.

"I gotta go," she said.

"Aww, M, don't be like that!" Noelle said.

Micah wasn't mad at them, but the longer she stood there, the harder it became for her to breathe. She thought of them seeing all of Milo's art, and how much better his was than hers. Their expectations of her when it came to Ty. The way Noelle had said, "Because of, you know, *Jesus*," like what Micah had been raised to believe was stupid. Like deciding to have sex was something *easy*.

"Stay up here if you want," she said. The four of them had spent enough time on her roof that they could show themselves out. "But make sure you close the door when you head back downstairs. And don't forget anything. I won't be back up here tonight."

"You're late," her father said as she squeezed into the pew to sit down beside him.

"Only by a few minutes," she started to explain. "The girls were on the roof and—"

"I know. It's fine. Just don't let it happen again, all right?"

He didn't look at her as he said it, so she knew there would be hell to pay later. She could tell by the slant of his head and the way he avoided her eyes that he was annoyed about more than her being late. He wouldn't tell her why while they were here, though. Her father was not a man who made scenes.

"I'm sorry," Micah said softly. But he had already turned away from her.

Her mother leaned over and kissed her on the cheek, folded down Micah's collar, and smoothed it with her hand until it lay flat.

"Honey, why is your mouth blue?" she whispered.

"Ice pop," Micah answered, and her mother shook her head and smiled.

"Maybe skip that next time if it's this close to when you'll be attending church."

Micah nodded as she pulled her Bible from her bag. "Is Daddy mad at me?"

Her mom pressed her lips together tightly and scooted a bit closer to her daughter. "Well," she whispered, "Sister Patrice called us.

She said you and Ty have been disappearing at camp during lunch, and yesterday she caught you kissing in the back parking lot."

Micah's breath quickened. She glanced sideways at her dad, but he was watching Pastor Bridges as he paced across the pulpit.

"I understand. You like him. You're a teenager. These things happen. But your father is . . . not happy. To say the very least."

Sometimes her mother could convince her father to be sensible. Like the time Micah lost her brand-new cell phone, or the one time she skipped a class (and got caught). But when it came to his feelings about boys, her father rarely budged.

"Oh," Micah said. She knew she'd get an earful the second they got home, so she tried to enjoy her last few hours of peace.

As she sat in the wooden pew between

her parents, Micah held her Bible in her lap. It felt as heavy as a stone. Unlike the Bible she'd found in Milo's drawer, which was dog-eared and all marked up, the pages in this one were still crisp because she only ever opened it during service. It made her feel guilty, like she was letting someone down.

She bowed her head and tried to listen as Pastor Bridges prayed, but she kept thinking about Ty. That made her feel guilty, too. She could see him sitting a few rows away. She lifted her eyes and let them linger on the back of his neck for a moment, until he turned and looked right at her like he'd felt her staring. He frowned and mouthed, *You good?*

Micah looked at her lap, then looked toward the pulpit, waiting for the next Scripture so she could flip to the right page and sink into the words. She would do anything to get away from how she felt when she looked at Ty, and the fact that they might be forced to wait after all, assuming her dad ever let her see him again.

5

"You and Tyriq Valentine think you're grown, huh?"

They'd barely made it through the door of their apartment before her father laid into her about Ty and camp and kissing.

"No, Daddy. Of course we don't," Micah said. She hung her purse by the door and looked at her shoes.

"Coulda fooled me. Kissing behind church when you're supposed to be working sounds like the behavior of someone who thinks they're real grown."

"It only happened a few times, I swear," Micah said.

"Don't swear, Micah Nicole," her father answered.

"Yes, sir. Sorry."

"So, since you and Ty think you're grown, you can have some grown-up responsibilities for the next week. You'll only be spending money you earn, so hand over your credit card."

Micah gave this up willingly. She didn't use it much, only for things like movie tickets or the occasional new skirt when she went shopping with the girls.

"And hand over your phone, too, while you're at it, because I doubt you can pay this bill with what you make at that camp."

That hurt. Micah started to plead with her father, but one look at him told her she was fighting a losing battle. She pulled it out of her pocket, and her father had to almost pry it out of her hand.

"Speaking of camp—you'll still be going to work every day, but I'll be asking Sister Patrice to reassign you to the older campers. You clearly have too much time on your hands working with the four- and five-year-olds if you can sneak off with that boy. Idle hands are the devil's workshop."

Micah had begged to be assigned to the younger kids because they were easier—sweet-faced and kind, covered in finger paint and innocence. She wasn't looking forward to the ten- to twelve-year-olds, who were noisier and meaner and too close to her own age for her to effectively boss them around.

"And I think you'll be doing a few extra chores around here, too." This came from her mother. "While I don't think there's anything wrong with a little kissing—" Her father shot her mom a look, and Michelle Dupree shrugged and said, "What? I don't."

"United front, Shellie," her dad said a little under his breath, but Micah still heard. "We're supposed to be presenting a united front."

Her mother patted her dad on the arm before turning back to Micah. "But what I *do* have a problem with is you ducking your responsibilities at work. So maybe a little extra responsibility is what the doctor ordered. Make sure you're home by six. You'll be grocery shopping and helping me with dinner every night next week."

Micah swallowed hard then. "Even next Saturday?" she asked.

Her father finally looked directly at her; he'd been avoiding it since they'd gotten home.

Something in his face softened and he turned to look at her mother, who put a hand on her dad's shoulder.

Saturday was the anniversary.

"No, honey," her mother said. Michelle Dupree's normally silky-smooth voice now sounded more like a cracked vase or splintered glass. "We'll be doing something different on Saturday."

Micah nodded but didn't ask any other questions. "Okay. I'm really, really sorry. For everything."

In her bedroom, Micah spun in a circle with her eyes closed. Her flouncy skirt twirled around her like a spinning top and her short hair floated around her ears like wings.

She was crying, but something about spinning always made her feel better.

After getting into trouble, she DM'd her friends from her computer to let them know she was basically under house arrest until further notice. Tobyn had said *NOOOOOO* and Noelle had sent a row of laughing emojis. Lux had just sent *SMH*, and then, *Are your parents for real? If I was their kid, they'd realize how lucky they are to have you. I should have my dad call them.* They'd all laughed at that, and it had even made Micah smile through her tears. They canceled their plans to come to the roof tomorrow afternoon, and she told them she'd see them the following week, *when I get my life back.*

She DM'd Ty, too, telling him about what happened when she'd gotten home. *I probably won't see you as much at camp. My dad's gonna get Sister Patrice to assign me to another classroom.*

Boooooo, he sent. *Does this make you wanna put the brakes on what we talked about the other night? If this is what your parents do when you get caught kissing, I don't even want to think about what could happen if they caught us . . .*

No, Micah sent. *I think I still want to.*

Okay, Ty replied. *Then we'll figure something out. I'll miss you at camp.*

Micah put her headphones on and blasted her music, like Dr. Patel had told her to do when she felt like she might panic. While she felt a little sad to have let her parents down, she was mostly upset that she'd gotten caught. She didn't know how she'd make it a whole week, especially this week, without a cell phone. Micah already wished she could talk to someone, but she worried that her parents would take away her computer if they saw her on that, too.

She wiped her tears and peeked out into the hallway. Her parents were in the living room and the news blared loudly on the television. She tiptoed out of her room and down the hall. She pushed open Milo's door.

"They're mad at me," Micah said to her brother's empty bedroom. She'd brought the sketchbook with her, so she turned on the lamp beside his bed, opened the book, and peered down at it where it sat on her lap.

"I can't believe they took my phone," she complained. "Did they ever take your phone from you? No," Micah said, answering her own question. "No. Because you were perfect and never did anything wrong."

Micah had always liked church and

following the rules for the same reasons: Both gave her life order. They made things make sense. They quieted her anxiety because they made her feel like she had a little bit of control in an otherwise random universe. If she was good, if she followed the rules and made smart decisions and did as she was told, things would turn out good.

But when Milo died, Micah's whole world seemed out of control. Because he had always done everything right. He drew graffiti in his sketchbook instead of spray-painting the sides of buildings or subway tunnel walls. He attended Bible study and made straight As and applied to all the right schools. He'd never had a girlfriend despite being incredibly popular, despite everyone in the school wanting him. He'd focused on God and his grades and his art, just the way their parents wanted her to act.

"Was it worth it?" she asked him now. "Doing everything they wanted? Didn't you ever want to break the rules? Maybe you should have. Maybe you missed out, Mr. Perfect." He'd hated when she called him that.

She walked over, opened the fifth-story window, and leaned through. There were dozens of fireflies blinking on and off in the empty lot beside her building. It made the construction site look like it got dressed up for Christmas in July.

Soon a new building would block this view, and Micah longed to stop time so she'd always be able to see the world through this window as her brother had. "The neighborhood's changing," she said. "Everywhere I look, everything keeps changing." It wasn't fair that his life stopped but nothing else did. Micah felt her eyes fill with tears, and it made something deep in her chest ache for the sound of Ty's voice. In that moment, she knew she wouldn't be like her brother. She'd changed, too. And she was determined not to miss out on anything.

6

Micah was still grounded. But her parents allowed her to meet up with Lux for help with her senior project. Since Micah still felt pretty much at a loss about what to make, they'd decided to do something else to get their creative juices flowing.

"Like this?" Micah asked Lux.

"Yeah, but try to speed up," Lux told her. "The slower the ropes turn, the more likely you are to mess up. When you're jumping faster, it's easier to fall into a good rhythm. Watch."

Double Dutch. Lux told Micah it always

helped her clear her head, so Micah hoped it would do the same for her.

She'd helped Lux make it through an intense photography class this past school year, and at the end of it all, Lux had offered to teach Micah how to jump rope over the summer. This was her first lesson. Selfishly, Micah wanted to hang out with Lux because she didn't know much about Milo, and since she hates emotional stuff, Micah figured Lux wouldn't try to make her talk about how she and her parents planned to spend the anniversary (unlike Tobyn and Noelle, who had already DM'd her about it).

They'd tied one end of two thin cords to the fence at the park near Lux's dad's apartment and were taking turns turning the ropes and jumping. They switched spots again, and Lux jumped so fast, her legs seemed to blur. Micah wondered if she'd ever be as good as her friend.

Just then, an ambulance sped by on the street next to the park. Micah suddenly stopped turning the ropes and they slapped Lux in the shins, hard. "Hey!" Lux said. She leaned over and rubbed her legs. Micah had been hit with the ropes enough to know it stung. "Why'd you stop? I was on a roll!"

Micah tried to slow her breathing. Luckily, she could blame it on the heat, the fact that she'd been turning the cords so quickly, and that they'd been jumping rope all afternoon. Lux still didn't know about her panic attacks. "Can we take a break?" Micah asked.

"Sure," Lux said. She was out of breath, too, and she flopped down on the sheet in the grass they'd laid out next to where they were practicing.

Micah reached for her bag and pulled out a water bottle.

"Do you mind?" Lux asked. She was pointing to Milo's sketchbook.

"As long as you don't ask me about the anniversary," Micah said, sliding it toward Lux.

Since Micah had taken the sketchbook, she'd been keeping it close. She flipped through it on the subway and looked at it on her walks to church for camp. It was the first thing she grabbed in the morning, and she tucked it under her pillow at night. But she hadn't shown it to a single soul besides the time the girls grabbed it from her bag. She hadn't even mentioned it to Dr. Patel yet. Lux turned the pages slowly. Lux had a photography portfolio that she cherished almost as much as Micah loved Milo's sketches, so she knew how to handle art with care. It showed, the respect she had for the work in her hands. It made Micah feel good about sharing it with her.

"He was so good," Lux said, looking up.

Micah swallowed hard. "Yeah" was all she could say.

A comfortable silence settled over them as Lux kept flipping, and it continued even once she'd closed the book and handed it back to Micah. "Can I ask one thing?" Lux said.

Micah knew what she wanted to know, that Lux would ask what happened a year ago. But before Micah could say she didn't want to talk about it, Lux said, "Did he tell you what all the messages meant?"

Now Micah looked confused. "Messages?" Micah asked.

"Yeah. In his drawings."

Micah opened the book again. "What are you talking about?"

"Like that," Lux said, pointing to a page that she'd only seen for the first time that day but that Micah had looked at a few times before. Micah had never noticed, but at the bottom of the page was a line written in Milo's tiny, messy handwriting. It fit into the narrow space of the curb where line-drawn versions of her parents were standing in the portrait. It was easy to miss if you didn't know to look for it.

Would you still love me if I believed in art more than God?

"Whoa," Micah said. She flipped to the next page: a sketch of a dog playing in an open fire hydrant. The thick lines that made up the spray of water hid another message.

I wish finding joy was as easy as waiting for summer.

She flipped forward to the beginning of the book and saw that there were more messages hidden on almost every page.

I can't talk to my friends the way I used to

had been written along the edge of a page showing a bunch of little kids in a sandbox.

People always talk about losing time, but sometimes I think that time is losing me was hiding inside the drawn bricks of their apartment building.

"It's like he was using it as a journal," Lux said. "So he was, like, *really* emo, huh?"

Micah slapped her friend's arm. "Shut up. But yeah, it does look like it. I can't believe I didn't see these until now."

She and Lux looked at more of Milo's sketchbook and found hidden messages in almost every single one.

"I wonder what they all mean," Micah said.

"Why don't we find out?" Lux asked.

She pointed to a drawing of a boy with long dreadlocks leaning against a chain-link fence of a basketball court, the one closest to their apartment, laughing. Micah recognized him as Zero, Milo's best friend. The message on that page read, *You're a work of art.*

"Maybe we can ask *him.*"

Micah nodded, because it was a great idea. But what she was really thinking was, *I wonder if I knew Milo at all.*

7

TUESDAY, JULY 7, 4:00 P.M.

Dr. Patel: *How've you been feeling?*

Micah: *Good. No panic attacks in the last couple of days, so that's been nice.*

Dr. Patel: *Have you felt anxious at all?*

Micah: *Obviously.*

Dr. Patel: *That's to be expected, Micah. This isn't a one-stop shop to cure your anxiety. It's all about management.*

Micah: *I know, I know. I get it.*

Dr. Patel: *Your mother mentioned you'd need to use the office phone at the end of your session to let her know when you left. What happened to your cell phone?*

Micah: *Ugh.*

Dr. Patel: *Does that mean we shouldn't talk about it?*

Micah: *I may have gotten into a bit of trouble over the weekend?*

Dr. Patel: *I see.*

Micah: *They just expect me to be this perfect human. The second I do one tiny thing they don't expect . . . it's like the end of the world.*

Dr. Patel: *What was the one tiny thing?*

Micah: *I kissed a boy.*

Dr. Patel: *That doesn't seem like a punishable offense.*

Micah: *I know, right?! I may have kissed him when I should have been working.*

Dr. Patel: *Ah. At the church?*

Micah: *Yeah.*

Dr. Patel: *In front of small children?*

Micah: *Not like making out while they're watching . . . They were asleep.*

Dr. Patel: *. . .*

Micah: *What?*

Dr. Patel: [laughs] *Nothing.*

Micah: *You know, Milo would have never kissed a girl at work. Lately I've been wondering if he'd ever kissed a girl at all. And, like, what else he might have missed out on, just doing everything people told him to do.*

Dr. Patel: *Say more.*

Micah: *Well, I used to want to be just like him. When we were little, I would follow him around and literally do exactly what he did. I tried to dress like him. I wanted to* go wherever he went. And then, when he started making art, so did I.

Dr. Patel: But you love painting, no?

Micah: I do. But I started because of him. I went to Savage because of him. Sometimes I wonder if I got in because of him. My art's not as good as his.

Dr. Patel: From what you've shared with me, you're a beautiful artist.

Micah: But it's hard for me. It came easy to him. Like this project I need to do before the end of summer. I don't even have the beginnings of an idea. And I don't want to think about it. I want to think about Ty. I want to hang out with my friends.

Dr. Patel: Maybe it's okay to not want to work on your art constantly.

Micah: Milo loved his work so much; it's all he wanted to do. He was always drawing *and always going to church without complaining and always . . . being perfect.*

Dr. Patel: *You and Milo are very different people. And no one's perfect.*

Micah: *Yeah, I think I'm realizing that now. For instance, I'm already in trouble, so this will only make my life worse, but I'm not sure I want to go to Bible study tomorrow.*

Dr. Patel: *Milo never skipped Bible study?*

Micah: *Never. And it's not like I don't want to go ever again, I just have questions. I just need a break.*

Dr. Patel: *Have you talked to your parents about that?*

Micah: *Hell no. They wouldn't understand.*

Dr. Patel: *Okay. But why do you think you're holding yourself to this standard of perfection?*

Micah: *Because I'm still here. And Milo . . . isn't.*

8

"There he is," Micah said.

Lux shaded her eyes and went up on tiptoes to see. "Damn," she said. "He looks just like he does in the sketch."

Zero was playing ball at the courts like Micah knew he would be. He had his long dreads twisted back into a bun, and he'd taken off his shirt. His dark brown skin shined with sweat as he trash-talked another guy on the court like his life depended on it.

"Nah, I told you, you can't handle this!" Zero said as he dribbled around the kid he was playing. He took a shot and made it, nothing but net.

"A'ight, bet," the kid said. He grabbed the ball and jogged back over to where Zero was grinning, his shooting hand still hanging in the air. "Let's go again."

"Yo, Z," Micah shouted. When she used to come to the courts with Milo, no one would talk to her. But if she came alone, all the guys tried to get her number and she got tired of saying "I have a boyfriend" every five minutes. It felt weird being here without her brother beside her.

"Mike-Mike!" Zero said, using the nickname Milo always called her. He grinned big and walked toward her and Lux. "Where you been at, girl?"

"You know," she said. "Just around." They hugged and Micah introduced Lux to him.

"I'll be back, Jay," he said to the guy he'd been playing basketball with, and then turned back to Micah. "How you been, li'l mama?" His dark brows furrowed and he looked serious. "How's your heart?"

She smiled. She'd forgotten Zero always used to ask her that. They walked toward the fence and he kept an arm around Micah's shoulders.

"Been okay, I guess," she said. "Just keepin' busy."

"Yeah, me too. Courts ain't the same without him, though," Zero said. "Nothin' is." A second later, he asked, "Yo, is that his?" Micah remembered Lux was holding Milo's sketchbook. She nodded and he reached for it. "I haven't seen this thing in forever!"

Micah looked at Lux, who raised her brows. *Ask him*, Lux mouthed. But Micah wasn't ready.

"You know, sometimes when he met me over here, he did more drawing than playing," Zero said. He started flipping through the book and paused on a self-portrait of Milo. "I miss that skinny dude like crazy."

"You haven't really come around," Micah muttered, "you know, since it happened." Zero used to hang out at their place all the time, and Micah had known he'd be around less after Milo died, but she didn't think he'd disappear. She hadn't thought about it until Lux pointed to the sketch the other day, but she hadn't seen him in months.

"I wanted to give you guys some space," Zero said. "Plus, me and him didn't end on great terms, you know?"

Micah frowned. "No, I don't know."

Then Lux said, "What do you mean, *end*?"

Zero untwisted the T-shirt that he'd tied to

the fence and pulled it on.

"We broke up at the beginning of last summer. We had just been getting back to a good place—to where he was coming around the courts and we were hanging out again—when everything happened."

"Wait," Micah said. "You and my brother were together?"

"Like, *together*-together?" Lux echoed.

Zero grinned. "You knew that, Mike-Mike! All the times we hung out till late? All the days we'd be gone for, like, hours at a time?"

Micah shook her head slowly. "I didn't know anything about that, Z."

Lux whispered, "Holy . . ."

"Wow, really? I knew your moms and pops didn't know about us, but I thought you and Milo were close."

"We were," Micah said like a reflex. "I mean,

I thought we were, too."

Micah flipped to the sketch of Zero and pointed to the hidden message. "Did you know he hid messages like this in his sketches?"

Zero took the sketchbook, pulled it closer to his face, and squinted at the tiny text. "Whoa," he said, and then, "Nah, I didn't."

"You're a work of art?" Lux whispered to Micah. "That's romantic as hell, now that I think about it."

"Yeah," Micah agreed. "It is." And if she missed something as obvious as that in Milo's messages, what else hadn't she seen? "Why didn't he tell me about you? I mean, what was really going on with you two?"

"I . . . think he was just afraid."

The thought that her brother could keep such a big part of himself hidden from her made Micah's chest ache. She thought about how Milo had never had a girlfriend, never paid girls much attention at all, and things started coming together bit by bit in her head.

"What did he think I'd do?" she asked.

Zero looked at his feet. "I just know he didn't want your parents to know. He wasn't ready to tell them yet."

Micah nodded. But it still made her sad.

Micah flipped back to another sketch, a glass of water on a messy table, and she looked at Zero and pointed to the message.

"Do you know what *Maybe it's not half empty or half full* means?"

Zero slowly shook his head. "No clue."

Micah turned the page. "What about *Sometimes the sound IS the fury*?" They were looking at a sketch of a pair of headphones, the cord split and the wires unraveling.

Zero shrugged. "I'm sorry, Mike-Mike. I wish

I could be more help. Truth is, your brother wasn't the most open person, even with me."

Micah flipped to another page in the sketchbook and then another. If she really knew her brother as well as she thought she had, she should at least be able to guess what these messages meant. But the words all just seemed to be puzzles that were impossible to solve. She felt tears prick at the backs of her eyes.

Then Lux spoke up. "Micah. What if they're all secrets? What if he wrote them this way so no one would ever know what they meant?"

Micah shrugged. "Maybe."

"I mean, I'm sure there are things Milo didn't know about you."

She knew Lux was right. But it still hurt that he hadn't trusted Micah enough to share his secrets with her.

Micah turned one last page and landed on

a sketch of a beat-up pair of sneakers. It took a while for Micah to find it, but the message had been written along the length of one of the laces.

It read, *We're all running scared.*

9

It was happening again. But this time Ty was with her.

Micah knew the over-ninety-degree temperature and the unbearable humidity were to blame. But her racing heart, her sweaty palms, and her breath did not care about the reason.

An old woman with fluffy white curls lay right there on the sidewalk, her bag of groceries spilling into the street beside her. She'd passed out on the corner next to the grocery store where Micah was doing her parentally enforced shopping. An ambulance was half a block away, stuck in traffic, siren roaring.

"I have to get out of here," Micah said to Ty, trying to keep her voice level. They'd been laughing a second ago, since Ty had been working hard to keep her mind off of all her brother's secrets. But now he looked worried, and Micah didn't know how much longer she could hold it together.

"Okay," Ty said. "Let's go."

They were only a few blocks from her apartment, but the grocery bags were heavy, and she needed to walk in the same direction as the ambulance to get home. "Where are you going?" Ty asked. He'd come shopping with her to help her carry what she needed to buy. He lifted his hand and pointed in the direction of her building. "Don't you live this way?"

Micah nodded and stopped moving.

She tried telling herself everything would be fine. She tried slowing down her breathing.

"Micah, what's wrong?" Ty asked.

"Nothing, let's go this way instead." She walked as quickly as she could away from the siren, but even on the next block the sound was deafening. Nothing was working.

She sat down at a bus stop shelter and dug through her bag, desperate for her headphones. She found them, and then dug deeper, looking for her phone. Micah had tried to turn her head away from the fallen woman as quickly as she could. But now she couldn't erase the image from her mind of the woman lying there, leg twisted at an odd angle. Micah thought that if she could turn her music up loudly enough, she could at least silence the wail of the ambulance and keep her head down until it passed.

She knew Ty was watching her, but Micah

overturned her bag, losing patience as the sound of the siren got louder—traffic must have creeped forward just enough to make things worse for her. She shoved aside her wallet and the sketchbook, her sunglasses and lip gloss, her water bottle and raspberry-scented lotion. And then she remembered: She didn't have her phone. She still had to serve a few more days of her weeklong punishment, so the phone remained turned off and locked away somewhere in her parents' bedroom.

"Oh my God," she said. The panic rose in her until her throat was so tight, she thought she might pass out just like the woman in front of the grocery store. Wouldn't that be ironic? Someone calling an ambulance *for her*, thinking it would help, but really they'd be bringing her biggest fear directly to her. The thought made all the muscles in her shoulders clench and her hands go numb. She needed to drown out the noise, but she couldn't play music like Dr. Patel had suggested. She needed to call Noelle, but that wasn't possible, either. And she couldn't walk home because she could hardly breathe, let alone stand and put one foot in front of the other.

"Hey," Ty said, putting down his bags. "Hey, what's going on? What do you need? What can I do?"

She thought of Milo then. Of his accident and last summer and that the coming weekend would mean she'd spent a whole year without him. Tears filled her eyes and spilled over, and when Ty asked again what he could do, all she could say was "Please don't call an ambulance."

She thought she might puke. Still trembling, she bent over and shut her eyes tight.

When Ty reached out, she let him hold her.

And a dozen minutes later, once it was over, she opened her eyes and looked up at him.

"Micah, you're scaring me. What just happened?"

He bent and started to put everything back into her purse. He righted the grocery bag and picked up the loaf of bread that had fallen out.

Micah laughed a little. Then she sobbed. He wrapped her in a hug and pressed his lips into her hair. "It's okay," he said. "Shhhhh, it's okay."

Once she'd calmed down, she told him the truth. It wasn't like she could hide it anymore. "I . . . have panic attacks sometimes. It's ambulances that trigger them usually. The siren reminds me of Milo's accident."

"Micah," he said. "That . . . really, really sucks."

It was the best way he could have reacted. She laughed and wiped her tears and wondered what she'd been so worried about.

"It really, really does," she said.

"Let me walk you home," he replied, like nothing at all had changed between them. He looked up at the graying sky. "It looks like it might rain."

"Thanks, but I think I got it." Micah pulled out her umbrella.

"You sure?" he asked. He touched her cheek and she nodded. She appreciated his offer, but something about telling him, simply saying it out loud, had made her feel better. Stronger.

"I'm sure. Thank you," she said back.

It started to rain just as she kissed him goodbye.

"You're late," her father's voice boomed the second she walked into the apartment.

Micah dropped the groceries on the kitchen counter with a thud and closed her wet umbrella.

"Careful," her mother warned. "Aren't there eggs in there?"

Micah didn't reply to either of her parents. She could only think about Ty and ambulances, the hot day that ended with pouring rain, and the woman who had fainted. Then she thought about Milo and his secrets. Wordlessly, she started putting the groceries away, making sure to leave out all the ingredients for the pork chops and black-eyed peas she knew her mom wanted to make for dinner that night.

"Micah," her father said. "Why are you just getting home?"

It didn't matter what she did, she realized. She'd never be Milo. And though they didn't say it out loud, she knew her parents were silently and constantly comparing her to him, despite not really knowing him at all. Milo's art was effortless. Milo would never make out with someone while on the clock at a summer job. Milo didn't have anxiety.

"I was with Ty," Micah said, instead of any of the other things she could have.

Her father looked surprised and then angry. He let out a sarcastic laugh. "You're pushing your luck, Micah Nicole," he said.

Her mother turned to face her. "Wait, really?"

"Yes. I love him," Micah said. "He loves me, too."

Her parents looked at each other.

"Oh, and I had another panic attack," Micah said. Since her parents sent her to therapy and picked up her medication, they considered her anxiety taken care of. And Micah had maintained the lie that she was fine. But she wasn't. And the closer they got to the anniversary, the more obvious that fact became.

"Oh," her mother said. "Are you all right?"

Micah shrugged.

"I thought Dr. Patel had given you a new prescription. Are you taking it every day like you're supposed to?" her dad asked.

"I am, but it's not like a cast fixing a broken arm, Daddy. It's the way my brain works. It's complicated."

"I think you need to take a break from seeing Ty," her father said next.

"What? Why?"

"At least until you get these fits more under control. You have a lot on your plate. Maybe you need to see a different doctor. I don't know what we're paying him for if this is still happening."

Micah felt herself getting angry. A strange kind of fire began building in her chest.

"What the hell? *Fits*? Seriously, Daddy? If you want to know the truth, it got really bad today because I didn't have my phone. I couldn't do any of the things the doctor told me to do when I feel one of my 'fits' coming on! I couldn't call a friend. I couldn't listen to music. But Ty was there for me today. Which is more than I can say for you."

Micah didn't know where the anger was coming from, but it felt like jet fuel in her blood.

"Micah!" her mother said. "I don't know what's gotten into you, but I think I agree with your dad. Taking a break from Ty sounds like a good idea. Get to your room, and I don't want to see or hear you until breakfast."

10

"My parents are going out of town tonight," Ty said. "Too bad you're still grounded or now would have been perfect."

"Let's do it tonight, then," Micah replied. "Grounded or not."

Even though she was working with the older kids now, they'd still been able to sneak away at camp again, but not to the back parking lot this time. They'd found an empty prayer room, one that hadn't been taken over and used as a camp classroom. As Micah grabbed both of Ty's hands and insisted tonight be the night, they heard a noise in the hall that made them move farther away from the door.

"Wait, Micah." Ty laughed. "I wasn't serious. You're *grounded*, and the whole point of us waiting and making a real plan was so we wouldn't get caught. Do you really want to piss your parents off more by staying out past your curfew?"

"They don't have to know," Micah said. She'd been thinking a lot about how best to make this work.

"You don't even have a phone right now. And isn't tomorrow the anni–"

"None of that matters," Micah continued. "I'll just wait until they're in bed. It'll be easy. I've never snuck out before, so they won't expect it. My dad's gonna pass out the moment he gets home because he works late on Fridays. And my mom is a light sleeper, but I'm sure she'll have a glass of wine or two tonight because of . . . what tomorrow is."

"I don't know . . . ," Ty said. "Won't you be, I don't know, really sad tonight?"

Micah swallowed hard as her chest tightened with panic. She couldn't tell if she was afraid of what she might feel tonight, afraid of what it might mean if Ty didn't want her the way she wanted him, or both.

"Wait. Are you not sure about me? About this? I don't want to pressure you into doing something you don't want to do."

"No. It's not that at all. You know how I feel about you, Micah."

He stepped closer to her and kissed her hard and long.

"Okay, so meet me tonight. At eleven," Micah said. And when he still looked unsure, she added, "When will we ever have another opportunity like this one?"

Ty shrugged.

"Exactly. So let's do it."

Ty agreed, and he grinned. Then he scooped Micah up and spun her around.

Ty was right. Micah didn't have her phone. But she had to tell her friends about their plans. After she helped her mom make dinner, she slipped into her bedroom and opened her computer. She hoped they were around.

It's happening tonight, she sent. *He's meeting me and I'm going to sneak out and I'm scared but excited.*

Whoaaaaa, Lux sent.

Seriously? Tobyn asked.

I'll believe it when I see it from Noelle.

Tobyn chimed in again. *Wait. You're going to do it tonight? The day before the anniversary? Don't you and your parents have plans tomorrow? Aren't you guys doing anything to honor your brother?*

Micah didn't answer.

Oh yeah, Lux said. *I forgot it was so soon. Are you sure you want to do this now? Wouldn't you enjoy it more if you did it when it wasn't so close to such a sad day?*

I'm telling you. She's not going to go through with it, Noelle sent.

Micah had expected them to be excited for her, but they were ruining her moment.

I thought you'd be happy for me, she sent. No one replied for several long minutes, and Micah started to get mad. What kind of friends were they? She was already nervous, and their reactions were making her feel worse.

Right before she closed her laptop, one last message slid onto the screen.

Don't get caught.

Micah read Lux's final message and wished she could talk to her about this more. Lux had a past, had made mistakes and took chances. Micah wanted to ask her for tips on how to become more like her—daring and strong and unafraid. Micah didn't know if she could do this, what she should expect, or what to do to avoid getting caught. She'd always been a "good girl," after all, or at least that's what everyone always said.

But she'd been thinking a lot about all the secrets her brother had been keeping, all the parts of himself he'd been trying to hide. She decided she wanted to live her life out loud. Even so, she understood why Milo couldn't tell their parents about the boy he loved. It was the same reason she didn't want to tell them she wanted to have sex with Ty: She knew, just as Milo did, that they'd be disappointed. But Milo had so much more at stake.

It was almost ten, so Micah quickly hopped in and out of the shower, used her raspberry lotion all over her body, and brushed her teeth. She smoothed her hair in the mirror, put on her pajamas, and said good night to her parents. The second they turned off the TV and headed to bed, she changed into a tank top and a cute skirt and smoothed gloss over her pouty lips.

Here we go, she whispered to herself.

She waited another twenty minutes, and as soon as her parents were sound asleep, she crept down the hall and past their room. Milo's door was shut, and she slipped past it barely breathing, as if her brother were inside and she needed to keep her plan a secret from him, too.

Her palms felt a little clammy as she thought about what tomorrow would mean—a whole year without him—but she didn't allow herself to think about that for very long. She had somewhere she had to be.

It was so humid and hot outside, even without sunlight, that the air felt sticky and gross. But Micah didn't care; she ran down her block feeling wild and free. Ty stood waiting for her on the platform of the subway station closest to her apartment so they could take the train to his place together.

"Hey," she said. She walked up to him slowly and reached out to hold his hand.

"Hi," he said. "You look . . . good."

Micah blushed.

They boarded the next train that entered the station and barely spoke all the way to his apartment. As they climbed the stairs to his unit, Ty let go of her hand for the first time since he'd met up with her. He pulled out his keys.

"I didn't think this would be scary, since I'd be doing it with you," Micah said from behind him.

"Me neither," Ty agreed. "But I'm a little nervous." He stepped closer to her and kissed her slowly.

She wrapped her arms around his waist. "I am too," she said. "But I'm happy we're here."

His apartment was empty, just like she knew it would be, but Micah wasn't feeling nearly as confident as she'd felt when she'd imagined this moment. She followed him down the hallway that led to his bedroom. They stepped into the dark room, and Ty reached for the light, but she stopped him.

"I think it will be easier . . . at least for me . . . if we start things with the lights off," she said. Her voice wouldn't stop shaking, and neither would her hands. She sat down on his bed and stuffed her fingers under her thighs.

Micah thought she heard a tremor in Ty's voice when he replied, "Okay."

He sat down on the bed beside her and kissed her on the cheek. A rush of warmth made her neck and face so hot, she couldn't look at him, so she smiled and stared down at her bare knees. She held her breath and pulled her tank top over her head before she could talk herself out of it. Without thinking, she unbuttoned her skirt so that the hemline of her lacy underwear showed. Ty gasped a little and said, "Damn, girl," like she was doing something other than sitting there awkwardly in her bra and underwear.

He pulled off his shirt, too, and then they were touching each other again. He pushed a sweatshirt on the foot of his bed onto the floor before he cracked a joke about how he should have cleaned his room better. She laughed. She just about melted when he touched her neck. But something made her slow down as they inched closer to the center of the bed.

"Are you okay?" Ty asked her. Her breath suddenly started coming quicker than it had been a second before.

"I don't know," she answered honestly. She was alone in an apartment with the boy she loved, but she didn't feel 100 percent sure about what was about to happen. And she needed to be sure. "Are we rushing this?" she asked, pulling away from Ty.

He took a deep breath like he'd been running

and he needed to slow down. "If you think we are . . . ," Ty said. "We don't have to do more than this." He touched her face and kissed her neck, and she touched his cheek and kissed him back.

Her hesitation wasn't about disappointing her parents or even what she'd learned in church. Micah suddenly knew that being with Ty like this—with jokes and gentle touches, kisses and some of their clothes still on—was enough for her. She decided she didn't need to be with him in any other way. At least not yet.

"I like this," she said. "Just this. For now. Is that okay?"

Micah didn't think she imagined the look of disappointment on Ty's face. But a second later he smiled and said, "We have time. And I want to do it right."

They'd only been dating a few months, but

it felt like they'd known each other forever. Waiting a little longer didn't seem like such a crazy idea.

"Maybe we should watch a movie?" Ty suggested after they'd gotten dressed and kissed a bit longer. And Micah smiled and nodded.

When Micah heard Ty's phone ringing for the third time, she finally realized it wasn't a dream. She opened her eyes to find the sun shining brightly, and she sat straight up. She didn't even remember seeing the end of the movie.

"Oh no," she said, jumping out of Ty's bed. "No, no, no."

"Huh?" Ty asked, stretching and yawning.

He glanced at his phone and picked it up. "Hello?" he said sleepily. "Lux? . . . Yeah, she's here with me. Why?"

Micah grabbed the phone from him. "Lux?"

"Micah, your parents are freaking out," Lux said. "They must be calling everyone in your phone trying to figure out where you are. I didn't know you were gonna stay over!"

"I wasn't planning to! I guess we just fell asleep!"

Micah pulled the phone away from her face to check the time and saw that it was nearly ten a.m. "I gotta go," she said to Lux and Ty at the same time, and tossed him his phone. She grabbed her purse and ran out of Ty's apartment without looking back.

Micah's heart raced as she ran to the closest subway station, and her fingers felt numb as she swiped her MetroCard. Throughout the ride, she tried to calm her breathing, but she felt too tense and jittery. It was Saturday, July eleventh, and on this day last year, Milo had died. Micah had been pretending the day wasn't coming. But now the truth of it hit her like a freight train.

When Micah pushed open the door of her apartment, all was quiet and still. For one short minute she thought her parents might not be home, that she'd somehow escape their wrath, but then her mother poked her head out of her bedroom and into the hall. She held Micah's phone in one hand, and had the other hand on her hip.

"Where in the world have you been?" she said, and then into the phone, "Yeah, she just walked in."

That meant her father must be out somewhere, looking for her. That meant when he got back, she'd be in serious trouble. Again.

Micah expected her mother to yell at her, or to tell her how disappointed she was. But when her mom stepped closer to Micah, there were tears in her eyes.

"How could you?" she asked, her voice breaking. This, Micah thought, was so much worse than anger. "What were you thinking? Doing this today, of all days?"

"Mom, I—"

"I don't want to hear it, Micah. I've been going through your phone, calling every person in your contacts. Your father is driving around like a madman. I turned on the news, terrified something awful had happened to the only child I have left."

Her mother started crying then, and Micah closed the space between them, feeling full of guilt and sadness. "I'm so sorry, Mom," Micah said. She reached out to hug her and her mom reached back.

"You scared the crap out of me," Michelle Dupree whispered into her daughter's hair. "I wouldn't be able to survive losing you, too."

Things were calm between them for the twenty minutes it took her father to make it back home. When he arrived, he didn't say a word to her.

"Let's go," he said to Michelle without looking at his daughter. And even though she hadn't changed out of yesterday's clothes, Micah silently followed.

On the corner where Milo's accident happened, Micah's mother left a bouquet of daisies. Micah stared up at the museum steps where she used to meet him to draw, and then looked back at the busy intersection. Her parents stood there holding hands, and her mother wiped the tears from her eyes, but everyone else went about their business because they had no idea what had happened here.

Micah: *I snuck out, but I didn't actually do anything.*

Dr. Patel: *I bet your parents disagree.*

Micah: *I know. My dad's barely speaking to me.*

Dr. Patel: *Do you think sneaking out counts as doing something?*

Micah: *I meant, like, I didn't do anything sexual.*

Dr. Patel: *I'm not judging you either way, Micah. I'm asking. You snuck out, and*

were late coming home Saturday morning,
right?

Micah: *Yes.*

Dr. Patel: *Do you understand why your*
parents might be upset about that?

Micah: *I guess.*

Dr. Patel: *Why did you decide to sneak out*
that night? The Friday before the one-year
anniversary of your brother's death?

Micah: *I don't know.*

Dr. Patel: *You don't?*

Micah: *No.*

Dr. Patel: *Do you think the two might be at*
all related? That the choices you've made
lately were all about control, right when
you were feeling the most out of control
you've felt in a year?

Micah: *. . .*

Dr. Patel: *Micah?*

Micah: *Maybe.*

Dr. Patel: *Right when you were trying to avoid being reminded of the most painful event in your life?*

Micah: *. . . I don't want to talk about it.*

Dr. Patel: *Okay. I understand. And we don't have to. But I'd like you to really consider the timing of all of this. I'd like you to ask yourself some hard questions and think about what might really be going on.*

12

Micah went to visit Zero again, this time on her own. She didn't really want to talk to anyone about Milo, but being with Zero just made her feel closer to her brother somehow. Maybe it was because Milo loved him, and love like that can leave a mark. She took the sketchbook with her, and when she got to the courts, Zero looked like he might be leaving.

"Hey, Z," Micah said.

"Hey, Mike-Mike," Zero said. "How's your heart?"

"I could ask you the same thing."

The wind was blowing hard, so the weather felt breezy and lighter than it had in the past few weeks. Micah had to keep fixing her hair and holding down the flouncy floral skirt she had on.

Zero looked sad for a second before he said, "Yeah, Saturday was rough."

Micah nodded. "It was for us, too."

Zero grabbed his bag and tucked his basketball under his arm. "I was just about to go somewhere. You wanna come?" he asked her.

"Sure," Micah said. She didn't even ask where they were going.

They walked through the rest of the park where the courts were, past the corner store, and farther down the block. They kept walking through their East Harlem neighborhood, and as they passed Augusta Savage School of the

Arts, Zero started to talk about Milo.

"Yo, this one time, your brother tried to teach himself how to skateboard with my board, and he kept eating it. He fell, like, eighteen times in an hour. But he kept getting back on and doing it again. I swear he was trying to ollie, but he never really figured it out."

Micah shook her head. "That sounds like him. He could be so stubborn, and he thought he had to be good at everything."

Zero said, "I know, right? We used to get into these heated arguments about the dumbest stuff. He was such a know-it-all. He always had to be right."

They were still walking. Zero seemed to know exactly where he was going, so Micah just kept following his lead. They passed a guy with a bubble machine on the corner, and little, smiling kids were chasing dozens of the shiny bubbles down the sidewalk.

Slowly, Micah began to talk, too.

"What was that song he was always whistling?" Zero asked.

"'Amazing Grace'?"

"No, the other one."

"Oh, 'Get Ur Freak On.'"

Zero started laughing. "Yep. But just like the opening notes, right?"

Micah laughed, too. "Yeah. Those same, like, six notes over and over again. It drove my mom crazy."

They were almost at the Harlem River when Zero pointed to a bridge and then to a narrow space under it.

"We're going right down there. Be careful," Zero said.

The underside of the bridge had been completely covered in bright, wildly painted graffiti. There were hard-to-read tags in a rainbow of colors, images of everything from soda cans to huge faces, messages written in curly script, and more.

"Whoa," Micah said.

"Yeah," Zero replied. "Me and your brother used to come here all the time."

"Did he ever paint anything here?" Micah asked.

Zero nodded. "But it's been painted over already. That's why he liked doing it here. He liked that he could play around and just have fun. Be imperfect. He knew it wouldn't last."

They stayed under the bridge talking and looking through the sketchbook until Micah had to head home. She was grounded again because of sneaking out. But before she left, Zero asked if he could hold on to the sketchbook for a while.

"Of course," she said. And as she walked away, she noticed a spray-painted image of a bright white bike with wings flying over a miniature NYC.

It gave her an idea.

13

That weekend, Micah invited Noelle over. They worked on their senior projects together on the roof. Noelle worked on mastering the final notes of her cello solo as Micah painted.

"Your parents still pissed?" Noelle asked after they'd been working for a while with only the sound of her cello passing between them.

"Yep," Micah said. "I think they will be forever."

"Probably," Noelle agreed. "How's Ty?"

"Pretty okay. Maybe kinda disappointed. But he's not being a dick about it or anything."

"How'd you get the idea for this?" Noelle asked, gesturing toward Micah's work.

"Zero," Micah said. "My brother's friend. Well, actually, I just found out he was more than his friend. But he's great. I've been hanging out with him a bit, and I think he'll like it. I'm going to set it up next Saturday. Zero will be there. You and the girls can come."

"Wait. What do you mean, *more than* his friend?"

"They dated. Milo loved him, but he wasn't ready to tell me or our parents. That's all I know."

Noelle didn't say anything for a long time, so after a bit, Micah asked, "Is everything okay? Like with Pierre and the restaurant and stuff?"

"We're fine," Noelle said, a little too quickly. And then, "I knew you weren't going to do it."

Micah didn't know why, but Noelle's

comment pissed her off much more than it normally would. She started to ignore it, but instead she said, "I don't know what your problem is with me lately. All the low-key mean stuff you say is really starting to get to me."

Noelle didn't look away from the sheets of music in front of her. She erased something and scribbled something else down. "It's just that, you're so worked up about Ty when the anniversary of your brother's death just happened. I mean, if anything ever happened to Pierre, I wouldn't give two shits about some random dude."

Micah felt her eyes instantly fill with tears.

"Is that what you really think of me?" Micah asked. "That I don't care about my brother?"

Noelle finally looked at her.

"Actions speak louder than words."

Micah started packing up her stuff. She didn't know why Noelle would say something like that to her, but she wouldn't stick around and figure it out.

"You know what, Noelle? You're so judgy when it comes to everyone else. But have you ever taken a moment to look at yourself?"

Micah saw Noelle clench her jaw, and something in Noelle's eyes softened. "Micah, look–"

"No. *You* look. You act like you know what it's like to lose someone. You act like you get it. But you never ask me, Noelle. You haven't asked me how I'm doing or what I'm feeling or if I'm okay. You've only judged me for reacting to something awful in a different way than you think you would. The worst part? You know how bad it's been because you've seen some of my worst panic attacks. You should be the last person to judge me like this.

"And you're right." Micah couldn't stop crying now as she stood at the door to exit the roof. "Actions do speak louder than words."

Micah: *I always hated that bike.*

Dr. Patel: *. . . Milo's?*

Micah: *Yeah. He rode it everywhere, though. To work, to school, to his studio and back home. Over bridges and through parks, and once he rode all the way to New Jersey.*

Dr. Patel: *Sounds like he loved it.*

Micah: *Yeah, he did. It was bright yellow. And Milo put stickers all over the seat.*

That's actually how I knew. Before I even saw the shoe, I knew it was him because of that seat.

Dr. Patel: *Do you want to tell me what happened? I think it would be helpful, just to say it all out loud. You never have before, right?*

Micah: *No. Not even to my parents.*

Dr. Patel: *Only if you're ready. But, Micah, you can do this. You're stronger than you think.*

Micah: [sniffs] *Okay.*

Dr. Patel: *Okay.*

Micah: *Okay, so I saw the seat. Then I saw his red shoe. It had flown off, I guess from the force of the car hitting him, so it landed across the street.*

We were meeting at the museum because we both liked to sketch the people sitting on the steps. Milo was better than me at it, so he'd always give me tips and show me different ways of looking at things.

Sorry, I'm going out of order.

Dr. Patel: *It's okay. Take your time.*

Micah: *Okay. It was hot and I was rushing because I'd told him we'd meet at five, and it was almost five thirty. So when I came up out of the subway station, I stopped to pull a tissue out of my backpack to wipe some of the sweat off my face. I could hear the ambulance then, but I was looking down into my bag as I walked up the stairs. And I remember getting so mad because I couldn't find the tissue packet. The ambulance siren sounded really loud, but it's New York, you know? It didn't even faze me. I grabbed my water bottle instead and I unscrewed it. When I lifted my head* to take a sip, I saw the crowd and the ambulance right in front of the museum.

Dr. Patel: *How soon after that did you see the bike?*

Micah: *Well, I walked over just to see what was going on. I was hoping no one got hurt, but that street is so busy, you know? I figured maybe a pedestrian got hit or, like, two cars had crashed. I saw the bike when I got closer. Saw the seat. Then I turned and saw the shoe—the Jordans that he'd worked extra hours at the art studio to be able to buy on his own—and I put it all together. I shoved through the crowd and I started screaming.*

Dr. Patel: *What were you screaming? Do you remember?*

Micah: *"That's my brother." I couldn't stop saying it. I just kept yelling, "Move." "Get* *out of my way." "He's my brother."*

Dr. Patel: *I'm so sorry, Micah. What happened next? Do you want to keep going?*

Micah: *He was already in the ambulance, that's why they'd turned the sirens on. They were about to leave. So I got in with him. I don't think they were supposed to let me, since I'm a minor, but I was so hysterical that they couldn't stop me. Once I was in there beside him, though, I calmed down. I called my mom and dad. There were two people working on him at the same time, but I stayed calm. I just sat there until they were done and eventually I reached out and held his hand.*

The weirdest part was that he didn't even look that messed up. He had a black eye, and a bunch of scrapes and scratches, but he looked fine. Just like he'd taken a nasty fall or something.

The whole ride I was just calling him a dumbass, and even though he was unconscious, I thought he'd be waking up any second to tell me to shut up.

Dr. Patel: *But he didn't.*

Micah: *He didn't. He had . . . he was really messed up, torn up in ways I couldn't see. Brain damage and broken ribs. Internal bleeding and a bunch of other stuff I can't remember. He never woke up, and he died later that night.*

Dr. Patel: *And that happened a year ago.*

Micah: *Yeah.*

Dr. Patel: *And his room still looks the same.*

Micah: *Yeah.*

Dr. Patel: *And you have his sketchbook now.*

Micah: *I did . . . but I gave it to someone who was special to him. But he'd already started* *showing art at galleries. He was gonna go to SVA and make so much dope art. He was my best friend and, like, the best person in the world.*

I can't believe he's gone.

Noelle showed up early to help that Saturday morning. Micah wasn't expecting her, but when she arrived, with all her supplies, Noelle was already standing there with a big bouquet of daisies in her hand.

They got to work without speaking at first, moving together like they'd planned this as a two-person job all along.

"Pierre's been fighting again," Noelle said as soon as she found a moment that felt right. "He'd gotten in a fight the day before we were up on your roof, and I kept thinking, *What if* the other kid had a gun or a knife? What if they'd stumbled into the street while they were wrestling like dummies on the sidewalk? What if he gets arrested and sent to juvie? What if he dies? I still shouldn't have said what I said, but I'm just all freaked out about everything going on with him."

Micah nodded and gave her friend a small smile.

"I get that," Micah said.

"And the whole thing about your brother and Zero just had me buggin'. I don't know why."

"It's surprising, right? How someone could keep such a big secret?"

Noelle didn't say anything and Micah didn't push her. They moved closer to the edge of the curb, and as they finished up, Noelle took a step back. She reached into her bag and handed Micah an egg tart.

"Forgive me?" Noelle asked.

"Of course. But don't take your stuff out on me again. It's not okay, Noelle."

"I know," Noelle agreed. "It wasn't cool. I'm sorry."

By the time Micah's parents arrived, dozens of people lined the sidewalk, and they were all watching them. Zero, Tobyn, and Lux had shown up by then, too, and right in front of them stood Micah's final project.

Her parents walked around the bike slowly. "It's a ghost bike," Micah said. She'd seen them all over the city—bikes painted white and left as memorials for cyclists who were hurt or killed on the streets of New York. The one she made for Milo was spray-painted all white, the way all ghost bikes were, but Micah had painted some of the hidden lines of text from his sketchbook along the handlebars and pedals and across the length of the bike's body. She'd stuck daisies in the spokes and nailed a piece of wood with his name to the back of the seat. She'd covered the wood in stickers and pictures of him.

MILO DUPREE
ARTIST, BROTHER, SON & FRIEND
R.I.P.

Lux took a bunch of photos of the bike from all different angles, and Micah planned to get a few of the photos framed. Her mother started crying. Her dad just looked from the bike to her and back again. Micah had held on to a few of the extra daisies. She handed a small bundle of them to her mom.

"I'm sorry, for everything," she said.

"Micah," her father said. "You made this?"

She nodded.

"Oh, honey," her mother said. "It's beautiful."

"I was hoping you'd think so."

"I can't believe there's only a month left of summer," Lux said.

It was August first, Tobyn's seventeenth birthday. She'd told them she didn't want to do anything but hang out with them all day, so that's what they were doing. There were half a dozen balloons tied to the lawn chairs, and Tobyn was wearing a birthday sash and crown they'd grabbed at the dollar store. They all wore birthday hats like they were little kids.

"Micah, are you going to move the ghost bike? Like, take it to school to get your grade?" Tobyn asked.

"Nah, I'm gonna leave it there. Turn in one of Lux's photos, and if they want to see the real thing, I'll just tell them where it is. I want it to stay there forever," Micah said, thinking about the bridge art and how temporary it was.

"What are we actually going to do today, though?" Noelle said. "I'm bored."

Tobyn stopped cutting her cake and looked over at Noelle. "Excuse me," she said. "I think it's *my* birthday, not yours. And this is doing something."

But Noelle was right; they were all getting kind of bored, plus the rooftop was super hot.

"I have an idea," Micah said. "Follow me."

Micah led her friends down the streets of Harlem, past churches and schools, corner stores, and markets. Past old people, and little kids, and shirtless street performers dancing in the sun. They went to the bridge, and once they were in its shadow, Micah pointed straight up. They all looked at the graffiti with wonder until Noelle smirked.

"I think I know what we should do for our senior prank," she said. And all of the Flyy Girls grinned.

Ashley Woodfolk has loved reading and writing for as long as she can remember. She graduated from Rutgers University with a Bachelor of Arts in English and worked in book publishing for ten years. She wrote her first novel, *The Beauty That Remains*, from a sunny Brooklyn apartment where she lives with her cute husband, her cuter dog, and the cutest baby in the world: her son Niko. *When You Were Everything* is her second novel, and Flyy Girls is her first fiction series.

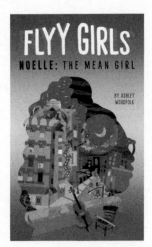